LOOK AND FIND®

Disney

Piglet

Cover character by Darrell Baker

Illustrated by Art Mawhinney
Lettering by Rich Koslowski

Written by Lynne Roberts

Visit our Web site at www.disneybooks.com

Published by
Louis Weber, C.E.O.
Publications International, Ltd.
7373 North Cicero Avenue
Lincolnwood, Illinois 60712

www.pilbooks.com

Manufactured in China.

8 7 6 5 4 3 2 1

ISBN 0-7853-7917-7

Publications International, Ltd.

As Piglet looks around the Hundred-Acre Wood, he is reminded that there are plenty of things smaller than he is. Look for these things that are smaller than Piglet.

ladybug

squirrel

haycorn

baby bird

frog

butterfly

inchworm

snail

pumpkin

If you want to learn to read and write, you have to know your ABC's. Help Pooh and Piglet practice their ABC's by finding at least one thing for every letter of the alphabet.

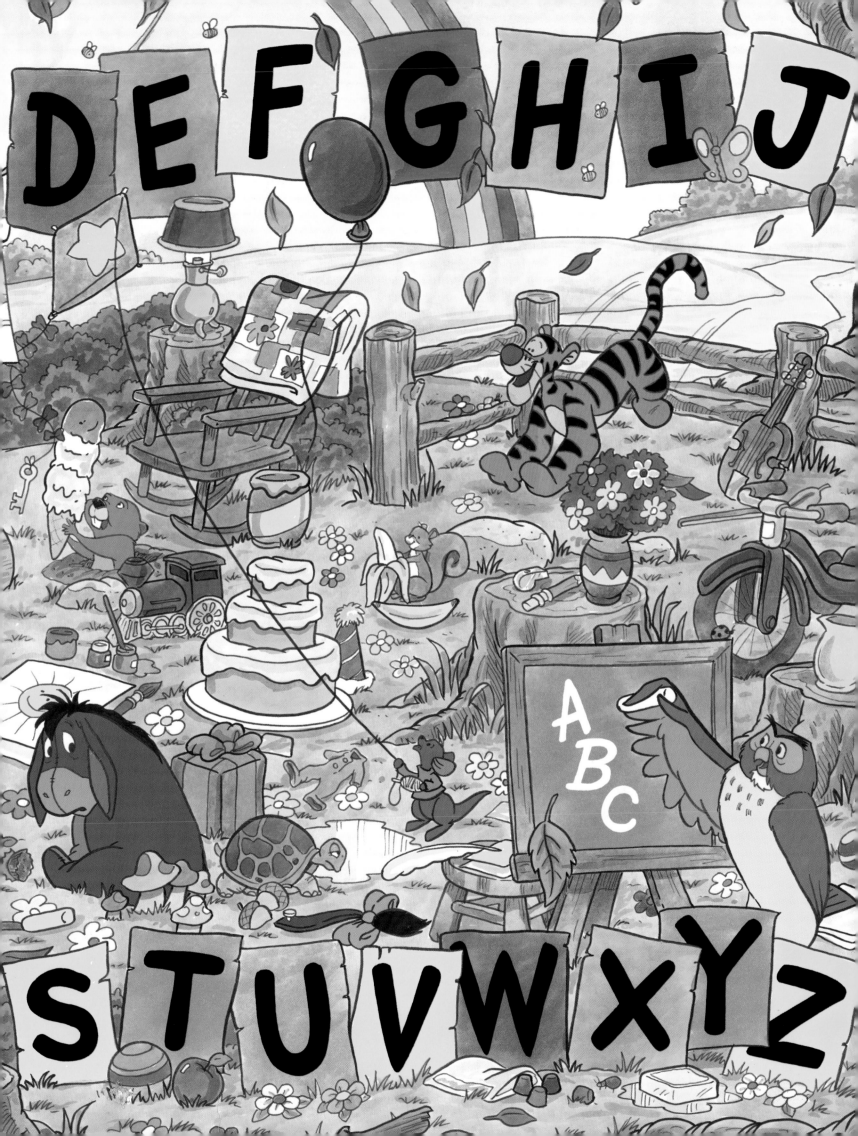

Piglet is amusing Roo by blowing bubbles with him. When the day turns blustery, the bubbles get a mite out of control! Look for these bubble shapes.

bubble heart

bubble star

bubble Piglet

bubble donut

bubble teapot

bubble haycorn

bubble flower

Piglet is still worried that he is too small to be very important. When he sleeps, he dreams of greatness. Look for these remarkable Piglets.

Sir Piglet

Captain Piglet

Professor Piglet

Piglet the Great

Detective Piglet

Mountaineer Piglet

Heffalump Tamer Piglet

Doctor Piglet

go PigLet!

It's fun to play Pooh Sticks, especially with your best friend. While Piglet and Pooh play, the sticks make great shapes. Look for these things.

Eeyore's house

A paintbrush

A sailboat

A wagon

A triangle

A star

A pinwheel

A butterfly

Piglet loves to draw, and he has taken his paints and crayons and created lots and lots of pictures. He wants each of his friends to have a special portrait. Look for Piglet's favorite pictures.

MY BEST FRIEND

MY BOUNCIEST FRIEND

THE FIRST TIME
I SAW KANGA

ROO LEARNS TO SWIM

RABBIT IN HIS GARDEN

OWL READS
A STORY

EEYORE IN HIS
GLOOMY PLACE

CHRISTOPHER ROBIN
MAKES MUSIC

SELF PORTRAIT

It's a snowy day in the Hundred-Acre Wood! Piglet searches the sky to find snowflakes that look alike. Help Piglet count the snowflakes, by finding:

2 of these

3 of these

4 of these

6 of these

8 of these

9 of these

11 of these

14 of these

Pooh? Tigger? Where is everybody? Piglet has found himself alone in the Hundred-Acre Wood, and he doesn't like to be by himself in such a big place. Help Piglet find where his friends have gone by getting through the maze.

Piglet's friends have dressed up like Piglet in his honor. They have decorated the Hundred-Acre Wood like Piglet, too! Piglet wants to thank all his friends for the party, but he's having trouble telling who is who. Look for Piglet and all his Piglety friends.

Pooh-let

Tigger-let

Owl-let

Roo-let

Kanga-let

Rabbit-let

Christopher Robin-let

Piglet himself

POOH AND PIGLET CORNER

Happy beeing me

Happy beeing me

Happy beeing me

Happy beeing me

Happy beeing me

Happy beeing me

Happy beeing me

Happy beeing me